Immortals

HERO

Ninja

Steve Barlow and Steve Skidmore

Illustrated by Jack Lawrence

Franklin Watts
First published in Great Britain in 2016 by The Watts Publishing Group

PB ISBN 978 1 4451 5104 5
ebook ISBN 978 1 4451 5119 9
Library ebook ISBN 978 1 4451 5120 5

1 3 5 7 9 10 8 6 4 2

Printed and bound by CPI Group (UK) Ltd, Croydon, CR0 4YY

MIX
Paper from
responsible sources
FSC® C104740
www.fsc.org

Franklin Watts
An imprint of
Hachette Children's Group
Part of The Watts Publishing Group
Carmelite House
50 Victoria Embankment
London EC4Y 0DZ

An Hachette UK Company
www.hachette.co.uk

www.franklinwatts.co.uk

How to be a hero

This book is not like others you have read. This is a choose-your-own-destiny book where YOU are the hero of the adventure.

Each section of this book is numbered. At the end of most sections, you will have to make a choice. Each choice will take you to a different section of the book.

If you choose correctly, you will succeed. But be careful. If you make a bad choice, you may have to start the adventure again. If this happens, make sure you learn from your mistake!

Go to the next page to start your adventure. And remember, don't be a zero, be a hero!

You are a ninja, trained in throwing weapons and hand-to-hand combat, attacking from the shadows with deadly accuracy. You live in Japan, which is ruled by the emperor and his war-chief, the shogun.

Your father was a samurai warrior, but when he was killed in battle your family fell upon hard times. You were too poor to become a samurai, so instead you have been trained in the ninja disciplines of silence and stealth.

Go to 1.

1

The moon is full as you creep towards the shadowed entrance to a temple. Your target is at the end of a wooden walkway, kneeling with his back to you.

You see from the uneven boards that you will have to cross a nightingale floor to reach your target. Each board is balanced so as to squeak a different note as your weight falls on it. You check your pack. You have hand and foot spikes for climbing, and mizugumo water shoes for wading across the surface of ponds.

If you want to use the spikes, go to 9.

If you would rather use the shoes, go to 21.

2

Using the evening shadows, you try to slip through the door, but a guard spots you. "Hey! You! What are you sneaking about there for?"

You cringe. "I meant no harm! I am only a poor minstrel."

"A minstrel should not be hiding in the shadows — I think you are a spy!" He calls to his fellow guards.

If you want to fight the guards, go to 41.
If you want to try to run, go to 18.

3

The captain of the guard is speaking. "The shogun's army is approaching," he says.

Raiden gives a scornful laugh. "The shogun will never take Gajo. I plan to lead an attack on his army before dawn!"

If you want to leave the castle at once and warn the shogun, go to 19.

If you decide to remain in hiding and find out more, go to 36.

4

You return to the main gates and conceal yourself in a position where you can spy on the castle.

The bandits supposed to be on guard are lying around snoring. The gates are massive and heavy. You decide to see whether you can open them without help — but it takes all your strength to move the gate even a fraction, and the noise you make awakens the guards. They draw their swords and rush towards you.

Go to 22.

5

"I wish to arrest Raiden," the shogun says, "but his castle, Gajo, is impregnable. I will not waste the lives of my men in a futile attack. You must find a way for my soldiers to get into the castle."

You bow again. "Order your attack on the castle for dawn tomorrow. I will make sure the gates are open."

As soon as the shogun has left, Master Iga hangs a pendant around your neck. "This is made from a dragon's tooth," he says. "Hide it beneath your clothes; but if you are in great danger, hold it in your hand and cry 'Return'. It will send you back to this time and place."

Go to 12.

6

You leap out of hiding and fight the guards, but they call for reinforcements. You realise that a lone ninja with only hand tools for weapons is no match for heavily armed warriors. They surround you, weapons raised.

Go to 22.

7

"If you want a fight, you can have one!" you tell the giant bandit.

The other bandits turn nasty. "No scabby minstrel challenges one of Lord Raiden's men!" cries one. The others roar agreement and pick up their weapons. They surge towards you.

You reach for your hidden weapons, but you are hopelessly outnumbered by heavily armed bandits. There is no way you can fight them all.

Go to 22.

8

You bow. "I am not worthy to share food with such brave warriors, but if you insist..."

As you share their food, the rude bandit says, "We need something to cheer up the warriors at the castle, minstrel. You will be welcome there."

You smile secretly to yourself as the guard leads you across the bridge. You have succeeded in getting through the outer defences.

Go to 34.

9

You put on the spikes. Silently you spider-climb the nearest wooden pillar and balance effortlessly on top of it. You spring from pillar to pillar, getting closer to the kneeling man with each stealthy leap.

You drop, as light as a feather, behind your unsuspecting victim and raise your hand...

Go to 33.

10

As you take the gunpowder barrels to the castle's main gate, you check the time by the position of the moon. You realise that it is too early to blow up the gates. Raiden will have time to shore up his defences before the shogun's army arrives at dawn.

If you want to put the gunpowder barrels into position and set a long fuse, go to 42.

If you decide to hide the gunpowder and set up a diversion, go to 35.

11

The captain leaves. You remain in hiding, but Raiden says nothing more. After a few minutes he summons a servant.

"Fetch me an oil lamp," he snaps. "I am going to bed."

If you want to try to capture Raiden as a hostage, go to 27.

If you decide to find the gunpowder store, go to 40.

You must reach Gajo before nightfall, but you cannot hope to get into the castle dressed in ninja clothing. You will need a disguise.

If you want to disguise yourself as a monk, go to 17.

If you want to disguise yourself as a minstrel, go to 29.

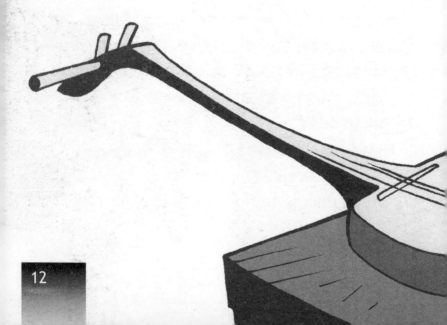

13

As you approach the doorway, you draw your katana and sweep the entrance from top to bottom.

Your blade slices through a hidden thread, setting off a booby trap. Hidden bows shoot arrows across the doorway. As they thud harmlessly into the walls, you step through.

Master Iga is pleased. "An expert ninja never drops their guard," he says.

Go to 25.

14

You make your way to a nearby village. As luck would have it, on entering a small inn you meet a miserable-looking minstrel.

"People here don't like my songs," he tells you.

"Well, let's do a trade, then," you suggest. "Try being a monk for a while."

The minstrel brightens up. "All right. It can't be worse than being a minstrel."

You swap clothes, and take the minstrel's flute and three-stringed lute. Then you head back to the castle.

Go to 39.

15

You sneak in behind the captain. He and the guard are checking small barrels of black powder.

"This is low-grade stuff," complains the man.

"It may be useless for firearms," says the captain, "but it will explode in a bomb..."

You try to creep nearer, but carelessly your foot scrunches down on some spilt gunpowder.

The captain turns and sees you. "Who are you? After him!" he cries as you run through the door — straight into the arms of a dozen guards, who seize you. You can barely move.

Go to 22.

16

You bang the gong with all your might. "To arms! To arms! The enemy is upon us!"

The bandits are thrown into confusion. Before torches can be brought, you slip away leaving the panicked men behind you.

You race back towards the main gate to set the gunpowder — and run full tilt into Raiden, who has been awoken by the alarm.

Go to 44.

17

Disguised as a travelling monk, you have a hard journey through mountain passes to Gajo Castle.

At last, you reach the outer wall of the castle — only to be stopped by Raiden's bandits guarding the bridge across the moat. One pushes you back. "We want no monks here!" he says roughly. "Be off!"

If you want to fight the men, go to 41.
If you want to try a different disguise, go to 14.

18

As the guards raise the alarm, you take to your heels. You find yourself in a courtyard full of Raiden's bandits, their slaves and their loot. Using your athletic skills to leap over sacks and flocks of bleating sheep, you outdistance the guards.

When the pursuit has faded, you find a storeroom over a stable. You are tired from your journey and you decide to wait for darkness to fall, and for the bandits to relax their guard.

You take off your minstrel disguise. You find some ground pepper in a sack and pour it into your flute. If you are taken by surprise, you can blow the stinging powder into your attacker's eyes. Then you settle down and are soon asleep.

Go to 43.

19

You retrace your steps, hoping to sneak out of the castle without being seen.

Unfortunately, you are spotted by guards who raise the alarm and give chase. Arrows whizz past you as you dive into the moat that surrounds the castle.

The chill of the moat water brings you to your senses. You can warn the shogun of the planned attack, but you cannot get back into the castle to open the gates. Your mission has failed. You will have to start again.

Go to 22.

20

You move instinctively, whipping out your pepper-filled flute. You point it at Raiden and blow.

Raiden howls, drops his sword and claws at his stinging eyes. You duck past him.

Reaching the gate, you take the barrels of gunpowder from their hiding place and put them in position. Seeing that it is nearly dawn, you set a short fuse.

Go to 26.

21

You put on the water shoes. These spread your weight so that you do not trigger the sensitive boards of the nightingale floor. You cross the floor silently and slip off the shoes. You creep up behind your unsuspecting victim and raise your hand...

Go to 33.

22

You reach inside your shirt and grasp the dragon tooth pendant. "Return!" you cry.

You seem to whirl through time and space. In the blink of an eye, you find yourself facing Master Iga.

The old ninja shakes his head sorrowfully. "You have made a poor decision. Begin your quest again — and choose more wisely in future."

Go to 12.

23

You laugh at the gigantic bandit. "I'd much rather sound like a frog," you say, "than look like one!"

The bandit raises his fists angrily, but the other bandits laugh and jeer at him, and he lashes out at the ones closest to him. A fight starts, and before long spreads throughout the hall.

You escape in the confusion and find a deserted storeroom above some stables. You are tired from your journey and decide to wait for full darkness and give the bandits a chance to calm down.

You take off your minstrel disguise. You find some ground pepper and pour it into your flute. If you are taken by surprise, you can blow the stinging powder into your attacker's eyes. Then you settle down and are soon asleep.

Go to 43.

24

You wait in the corridor until the guard captain and the other man come out. The captain puts his armour back on and they head down the corridor discussing the bombs the shogun has ordered.

When they are out of sight, you pick the door lock, sneak into the store and take two small barrels of gunpowder. You carry these out and lock the door behind you.

If you want to take the gunpowder straight to the gate, go to 10.

If you decide to hide the powder and start a diversion, go to 35.

25

Your Master, Iga, is now blind, but once he was one of the most renowned ninjas in Japan. A tall man stands in the shadows behind him, but your attention is caught by the presence of your cousin Aki, who is kneeling before Master Iga.

"Aki," you say, "why are you here?"

Aki wrings his hands. "I have come to ask for help. Our village has been attacked by bandits. The warlord Raiden sent them to burn our houses and steal our valuables. Even the rice harvest has been stolen."

If you want to set off at once to help the villagers, go to 37.

If you want to complain that the emperor has let this happen, go to 49.

Raiden appears. His eyes are streaming and he is very angry. He raises his sword and charges at you.

The gunpowder barrels explode. The gates to the castle are torn from their hinges. Raiden is hit by a flying piece of timber, and drops to the ground. The way to the castle is open, and you hear the triumphant war cries from the shogun's army as his men storm the gates.

Go to 50.

27

Unseen, you follow Raiden to his bedchamber.

You wait outside the door until you hear snores. You ease the door open and begin to creep across the room. But to your horror, you realise this is another nightingale floor. As you step on a loose board, a loud squeak sounds out.

Raiden is instantly awake, drawing his sword and crying for help. Guards enter with more lanterns and drawn swords. You can neither hide nor fight.

Go to 22.

28

The captain of the guard arrives. "A minstrel. I suppose you want to play for the men?" he says. "Well, you can sing for your supper — but I hope you're good. My men will eat you alive if you're not!"

The bandits are having a feast in the great hall of the castle. You play for them.

The bandits quieten down to listen, and at the end of the song they clap and cheer — except for one gigantic bandit.

"You have a voice like a frog!" he rumbles. He is clearly spoiling for a fight.

If you want to fight the bandit, go to 7.

If you want to make him look foolish, go to 23.

29

Disguised as a minstrel, you make your way through bleak mountain passes until you arrive at the outer wall of Gajo Castle.

A group of bandits guarding a bridge across the moat stops you. "What do you want, scruffy minstrel?" one asks.

If you want to fight the bandits, go to 41.

If you decide to try to talk your way across the bridge, go to 39.

30

You throw the stars at Raiden but they bounce off his armour or stick in the padding he wears underneath.

Raiden comes at you again, sword raised.

Go to 20.

31

You make your way to the great keep of the castle. You steal through silent corridors, making the most of your years of stealth training.

Hearing voices from a nearby room, you climb a wooden pillar to the next floor, and find yourself in a gallery overlooking the council chamber where Raiden is talking to his guard captain.

If you want to attack Raiden, go to 48.
If you want to listen to what Raiden is saying, go to 3.

32

You snatch a burning torch from the wall and turn the corner to confront the guards. "Good evening, friends."

The guards panic. "Take that thing away! Do you want to set off the gunpowder?"

"Is that what's in the barrels?" You bend down for a closer look.

The guards panic and run away. As soon

as they have gone, you get rid of the torch and remove the gunpowder.

Go to 35.

33

You tap your "victim" on the shoulder.

Your instructor, Bunta, turns and looks up. He smiles. "A most silent approach," he says. "I think there is nothing more I can teach you..."

He breaks off as a young apprentice appears and bows low. "Master Iga wishes to see you both immediately."

Master Iga is the head of the training school, a ninja of great power and knowledge. You wonder what he wants with you.

Bunta leads the way as you cross the courtyard, but when you reach the door to Master Iga's rooms, he steps aside so that you can enter first.

If you want to go straight in through the door, go to 45.

To check for hidden dangers, go to 13.

Inside the moat, Gajo Castle is gigantic, with great wooden fortifications rising from massive stone walls. You can see why the shogun thinks it is impregnable.

Darkness is falling as you walk up the winding streets between the mighty walls until you reach the main gate to the heart of the castle.

If you want to try to sneak into the castle, go to 2.

If you want to ask to see the captain of the guard, go to 28.

35

You hide the gunpowder behind one of the large silk banners that line the outer walls and head for the great hall. The bandits who were feasting earlier are still asleep and snoring loudly. Chairs and tables they have broken during a huge fight lie in pieces scattered all over the floor. They've clearly had a busy night celebrating!

You know that a distraction is needed so that the defenders' attention will be elsewhere when you blow up the gates. You spot a gong hanging at the back of the hall.

If you want to bang the gong to start a panic, go to 16.

If you want to gather wood from the broken furniture to start a fire, go to 38.

The shogun is an experienced general. You know he will have scouts on the lookout for Raiden's men. Your job is not to warn him of Raiden's plans, but to be ready to open the gates of the castle when he arrives at dawn. You decide to stay where you are and listen for more information.

"I am not happy about the gunpowder you have in store," the guard captain continues.

"The powder I have collected to make bombs?" says Raiden. "Why? What's wrong with it?"

"The men say it is not good quality."

"Go and check it yourself!" orders Raiden.

If you want to stay hidden and hear what else Raiden says, go to 11.

If you want to follow the captain to try to find the gunpowder, go to 46.

37

You bow to Master Iga. "I must go at once."

"Have patience," Iga tells you. "The emperor will deal with this outrage."

You are furious. "The emperor does not care for my village or he would send his war chief! The shogun would come to help us..."

"Your pupil is rash, Master Iga." The man in the shadows steps forward. You'd forgotten that he was there! "Perhaps you have chosen the wrong person for the task."

You recognise the shogun. You fall to your knees and apologise.

"I accept your apology," the shogun tells you. "But you must not insult the emperor!"

"I am sorry," you say. "Tell me what I must do."

Go to 5.

38

You gather wood into a pile and use the flame from a torch to set it alight. "Fire!" you cry.

The bandits wake up in panic. Most of Gajo Castle is made of wood — if the flames take hold, it will burn like tinder! The terrified bandits rush about, looking for water.

While they are busy, you race off to set the gunpowder and blow up the gates — only to run headfirst into Raiden, who has been woken by the noise.

Go to 44.

39

"May I go through to the castle?" you ask. "I am only a peaceful musician."

"Is that so?" The rude bandit winks at the others. "Let's hear you play, then."

You play your lute and sing a sad song about a young man and his lost love.

The rude bandit and some of the others are in tears. "That's beautiful," he says. "Come and eat with us."

To accept their invitation, go to 8.
If you would rather refuse, go to 47.

40

You search for the gunpowder store, but there are so many corridors and the guard captain has gone. Without him to guide you, you have little hope of finding the store.

As you wonder what to do, a guard spots you and calls for help. More armed guards come running, carrying torches. You cannot hide, and you cannot fight them all.

Go to 22.

41

You throw off your disguise and draw your hidden daggers. The startled guards attack, and you parry their clumsy blows.

But the guards call for reinforcements — there are simply too many heavily armed bandits! There is only one way to avoid your fate.

Go to 22.

42

You set the long fuse and go back to your hiding place.

But a passing guard sniffs the air. "I smell burning," he mutters. Then he spots the smoke from your fuse. Calling frantically for help, he snatches the fuse away from the barrels and stamps it out. More guards come running.

If you want to fight the guards, go to 6.
If you want to approach them with a lighted torch, go to 32.

43

You have trained yourself to wake up at any hour you choose. At midnight, you are instantly alert. You slip silently away from the storeroom and find that all is quiet in the castle.

If you want to check the castle gates and their guards, go to 4.

If you decide to find Raiden in an attempt to discover his plans, go to 31.

44

"A spy!" Raiden is already in his armour. Now he draws his sword and attacks you. You dodge his blows, but Raiden presses home his attack. "Stand still!" he shrieks.

If you want to use your flute to shoot pepper at Raiden, go to 20.

If you would prefer to use your shuriken throwing stars, go to 30.

45

As you step through the doorway, you feel a hidden thread break under the weight of your body. Instinctively, you sway back from the booby trap you have triggered. Hidden bows shoot arrows that pass a hair's-breadth from your chest. Your ninja reflexes have saved you!

Master Iga frowns. "Accept no place as safe," he tells you. "Always suspect danger."

You bow low and apologise for your mistake.

Go to 25.

46

You follow the guard captain down a maze of corridors until he arrives at a door guarded by a man wearing soft, loose clothing and slippers. The captain takes off his metal armour and also puts on slippers. You guess that this is to prevent sparks: you have found the gunpowder store!

The guard captain and the other man go through the doorway.

If you want to follow them in, go to 15.
If you want to wait until they come out, go to 24.

47

The rude bandit is suspicious. "No half-starved minstrel would ever turn down a meal!" His hand goes to his sword-hilt.

If you want to fight the bandits, go to 41.
If you think you should apologise and accept their food, go to 8.

48

You leap from the gallery to the floor, screaming. "You attacked my village! Die!"

You throw several daggers and shuriken stars, but Raiden and the captain fend you off, while Raiden bellows for reinforcements. Heavily armed guards burst into the room in overwhelming numbers. You cannot fight them all. Your recklessness has betrayed you.

Go to 22.

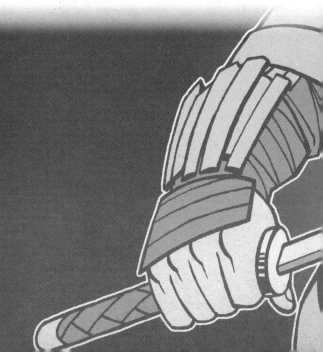

You are furious. "Raids on peaceful villages!" you storm. "Why has the shogun not come to stop these outrages?"

The emperor's war chief steps out of the shadows. "The shogun has come!"

You fall to your knees and apologise.

"I understand your anger," says the shogun, "but you must have faith in me — and in the emperor."

"I understand," you say. "Tell me what I must do."

Go to 5.

50

An hour later, the shogun's army has captured all of the bandits and is in complete control of Gajo Castle.

As Raiden is led away to answer for his crimes, the shogun thanks you. "You would make a fine samurai," he says. "I will sponsor your training, if you wish."

You shake your head. "My father was a samurai. I am a ninja. The emperor needs warriors who fight openly, in the light, but also those who fight secretly, in the shadows."

The shogun laughs. "Well spoken! Samurai or ninja, you are a hero!"

Immortals

HERO

I HERO Quiz

Test yourself with this special quiz. It has been designed to see how much you remember about the book you've just read. Can you get all five answers right?

To download the answer sheets simply visit:

www.hachettechildrens.co.uk

Enter the "Teacher Zone" and search "Immortals".

Question 1

What powder do you fill up your flute with?

A   gunpowder

B   paint

C   pepper

D   chilli

Question 2

What is the name of Raiden's castle?

A   Grino Castle

B   Gajo Castle

C   Grimy Castle

D   Jago Castle

Question 3

What animal does the tooth come from on the pendant Master Iga gives you?

A   dragon

B   shark

C   snake

D   tiger

Question 4

What type of warrior was your father?

A   a wokou

B   a yamabushi

C   an ashigaru

D   a samurai

Question 5

What time of day does the shogun attack Raiden's castle?

A   at midnight

B   at dusk

C   at dawn

D   at sunset

About the 2Steves

"The 2Steves" are Britain's most popular writing double act for young people, specialising in comedy and adventure. They perform regularly in schools and libraries, and at festivals, taking the power of words and story to audiences of all ages.

Together they have written many books, including the *Crime Team* series. Find out what they've been up to at:
www.the2steves.net

About the illustrator: Jack Lawrence

Jack Lawrence is a successful freelance comics illustrator, working on titles such as *A.T.O.M.*, Cartoon Network, *Doctor Who Adventures*, *2000 AD*, Transformers and *Spider-Man Tower of Power*. He also works as a freelance toy designer.

Jack lives in Maidstone in Kent with his partner and two cats.

Have you completed the I HERO Quests?

Battle with aliens in Tyranno Quest:

978 1 4451 0875 9 pb   978 1 4451 0876 6 pb   978 1 4451 0877 3 pb   978 1 4451 0878 0 pb
978 1 4451 1345 6 ebook   978 1 4451 1346 3 ebook   978 1 4451 1347 0 ebook   978 1 4451 1348 7 ebook

Defeat the Red Queen in Blood Crown Quest:

978 1 4451 1499 6 pb   978 1 4451 1500 9 pb   978 1 4451 1501 6 pb   978 1 4451 1502 3 pb
978 1 4451 1503 0 ebook   978 1 4451 1504 7 ebook   978 1 4451 1505 4 ebook   978 1 4451 1506 1 ebook

Save planet Earth in Atlantis Quest:

978 1 4451 2867 2 pb   978 1 4451 2870 2 pb   978 1 4451 2876 4 pb   978 1 4451 2873 3 pb
978 1 4451 2868 9 ebook   978 1 4451 2871 9 ebook   978 1 4451 2877 1 ebook   978 1 4451 2874 0 ebook

More I HERO Immortals

978 1 4451 4081 0 pb
978 1 4451 4082 7 eBook

Dragon

Steve Barlow – Steve Skidmore

You are the last Dragon Warrior.
A dark, evil force stirs within the
Iron Mines. Grull the Cruel's
army is on the march! YOU must
stop Grull.

978 1 4451 4088 9 pb
978 1 4451 4087 2 eBook

Mermaid

Steve Barlow – Steve Skidmore

You are a noble mermaid –
your father is King Edmar.
The Tritons are attacking your home
of Coral City. YOU must save the Merrow
people by finding the Lady of the Sea.

978 1 4451 4084 1 pb
978 1 4451 4085 8 eBook

Superhero

Steve Barlow – Steve Skidmore

You are Olympian, a superhero.
Your enemy, Doctor Robotic,
is turning people into mind slaves.
Now YOU must put a stop to his
plans before it's too late!

978 1 4451 3958 6 pb
978 1 4451 3961 6 eBook

Wizard

Steve Barlow – Steve Skidmore

You are a young wizard.
The evil Witch Queen has captured
Prince Bron. Now YOU must rescue
him before she takes control of
Nine Mountain kingdom!